Bible Dramatizations, Book 2

A Collection of Short Stories

C. J. Korryn

Published by C. J. Korryn Books, 2019

Bible Dramatizations, Book 2

Published by:

C. J. Korryn Books

****

©2019 by C. J. Korryn

****

Visit C. J. Korryn's website below for more of his books.

https://www.cjkorryn.com/books

Sign up for C.J. Korryn's newsletter

https://authorcjkorryn.wixsite.com/mailinglist

Table of Contents

Beautiful Gate

Peter and John walked down the streets of Jerusalem. They were heading to the temple to worship.

John was tall and slender, towering over Peter, who stood at shoulder level as they walked side-by-side. John had no defining features that set him apart from any other man. Peter, on the other hand, had a very distinct and prominent feature that all who met him never forgot. It was a testament to his rashness, both as a youth and even as an adult.

From his left eyebrow all the way down to the bottom of his jawline, he had a wide scar, a nasty, white scab of a scar against his dark tanned skin. No matter how thick he grew his beard, the scar could be seen as the wound couldn't grow hair, and his beard seemed to avoid covering his scar altogether.

He had the scar since he was a young boy. He was fishing with his father, and his father was teaching him a new way to fish. It wasn't efficient and an extraordinary waste of time as only one fish could be caught at a time rather than the dozens caught using nets. But his father said that some people who were not fisherman were starting to fish this way for recreation. As a boy, he could never understand how throwing a string out into the water and waiting for a fish to get caught on it was fun. He almost changed his mind when he caught a massive fish. His father had to help pull the fish in, and without thinking, Peter dove into the water ontop of the fish, the hook the fish was caught with slicing the left side of his face from eyebrow to chin.

John was a man easily forgotten as there was nothing significantly different or appealing about him to make him stand out from among the crowd of people. But Peter's scar ensured he would not be forgotten.

***

Jonas looked up at the sun, and the shadows then glanced down into his old, clay, cracked mug and frowned.

It was around three in the afternoon, and he had yet to make half of what he usually did begging at the temple gate.

He slammed the old, broken mug down, cracking it even more.

The sun had shifted the shadow he had been using for shade, and now, half of his body felt the heat of the sun. He grabbed his leg, lifting it and setting it back down a few inches over then did the same with his other leg, and then scooted over. He repeated this process until he had moved his entire body into the shade of the shadow.

He grabbed his mug and lifted it up as he saw a small crowd nearing. He didn't say a word, just held his cup up, not even bothering to lift his head.

He counted five pairs of feet but heard only one clang in his cup.

He did this day in and day out, sitting here in this very spot, since his family had died. His only means of survival now, the charity of those passing by, a meager means of survival.

He never bothered to look up anymore, realizing that the majority of the passersby simply ignored him. It was something he had gotten used to rather quickly, and now, after over twenty years of begging, he practically ignored them, as well. Not out of spite or malice but more because he felt it a waste of energy to look people in the eye who refused to acknowledge his existence.

He no longer cared to look up, and he no longer thanked those that dropped coins in his old cup, again realizing most people gave out of duty or obligation rather than compassion or caring about his plight. It was their religious duty to give—if they gave at all.

He just sat, lifting his cup, counting feet, moving with the shadow, day in and day out.

***

John walked with Peter, nearing the gate to the temple, and saw the beggar sitting there again. John had seen him many times but had never really taken notice of the man.

He slowed in his stride, losing himself in his thoughts, his eyes locked on the beggar.

Something rose up within him. A feeling he recognized but had never felt so intensely. He felt a sinking feeling in the pit of his stomach. His throat tightened, and he knew if he tried to speak, he wouldn't be able to. He wanted to cry but forced back the tears. He felt such sorrow, not for himself, but for this man who had been sitting at that gate ever since he could remember.

John wanted to help him, had to help him, but he didn't know what to say or how to help the man.

His palms began to sweat, and the feeling in his stomach morphed into butterflies. He knew, then, that the Holy Spirit was speaking to him about this man. He had felt the same feeling when he was in the upper room, after the Holy Spirit fell on him, and he began speaking in tongues, as they called it.

It was a sign that the Holy Spirit wanted him to do something.

He was mere feet away, and still, he hadn't a clue how to proceed, so he stopped and stared.

***

Peter noticed John slow and was about to say something to him when he saw the look on John's face. He was staring off as he walked with a blank stare, looking deep in thought.

Peter slowed, keeping pace with his friend and followed John's gaze. Peter understood John's countenance the moment he saw the beggar at the gate.

They were only a few steps away, and Peter could see the resignation to live a life of hopelessness in the man's eyes. He had seen the man many times over the years as Jesus had led them to the temple, but he hadn't paid much attention to the man before now.

He heard Jesus speak to him as John stopped next to the beggar. He heard Jesus more in his heart than audible, though his voice rang in his ears.

"Greater things than these will you do." He stopped, as well, looking at John, expecting him to say something, then seeing the teary-eyed, distraught look on John's face turned to the beggar.

***

Jonas still looked down at the pair of feet walking past, hearing no clanging of coins, then noticed two pairs of feet stop in front of him. Realizing they were contemplating giving him a coin, he lifted his cup a little higher. "Spare a coin for the lame?" he asked, still not bothering to look up.

"Look at us," he heard one of them say.

Suddenly, his heart fluttered. Few people spoke to him at the gate, but when they did, he always received a substantial gift. It was always the wealthy that spoke to him, so he knew he would get something great from these men.

He sat forward, looking at the two men, instantly noticing the large scar through the beard of one of the men, recognizing him as one the followers that walked with the one who was called Jesus. The one they put to death and who they said performed miracles.

"Silver and gold, I do not have, but what I do have I give you," the scarred man said.

Jonas' heart sank when Peter told him that he had no money to give. Delight transformed into despair as those words were spoken, his hopes for a warm meal that would fill his stomach, rather than the scraps he could barely afford from begging, shattered, and he sunk back onto the wall, letting his arm drop to the ground.

"In the name of Jesus of Nazareth, walk," the scarred one said, holding out his hand.

A tinge of hope crept back into Jonas' heart. He had heard about Jesus, though never met him. He knew all of the rumors surrounding this man and his followers. The rumors of Jesus' blasphemy, death, resurrection. He didn't know what was true and what was false, but he found himself clinging to this hope, this faith of Jesus' power. He had heard that Jesus could perform miracles, but he hadn't heard much about his followers' miracles.

***

Peter stood with his palm up for the beggar to grab. The beggar looked at him, then to John, and back to him.

Peter nodded, waiting for the beggar to reach out.

The beggar slowly lifted his arm, staring now at Peter's outstretched hand.

***

His heart raced as he lifted his arm; he felt it pounding in his chest and found it hard to breathe. He stared at the man's hand as he reached out, closing his eyes as he felt the warmth of Peter's hand.

He felt the man pull him upward, and he felt a warm

tingle in his feet as he tried to stand.

He didn't fall as he had so many times when he tried to

stand before.

***

The beggar stood to his feet, his eyes wide with

astonishment, and he began to walk. He stumbled, and John

reached out to steady him, then the man jumped up with a

scream. He jumped and walked back and forth with shouts of

joy.

A crowd began to gather at the entrance, watching this

man they all knew to be lame, walking and jumping.

The man kicked his cup, then screamed out in pain as the

cup clattered across the gate entrance, then he burst out into

laughter as he clutched his foot, balancing on one leg.

He jumped and hugged Peter and John, thanking them,

and praising God and the Jesus he was healed in the name of.

He took John and Peter by the hand, pulling them into

the temple courts, praising God.

"These two healed me in the name of Jesus of Nazareth. Praise God and praise to Jesus!"

He let go of Peter and John, who were now overwhelmed with joy, laughing and praising God with him.

The crowd had followed them in from the entrance, and those inside now gathered around this crazed man jumping and laughing and yelling praises to God.

Peter saw an opportunity to preach the name of Christ and stepped forward, resting a hand on the beggar, who quieted down, and Peter began to proclaim the name of Jesus to the awed onlookers.

The Light

A hooded figure inched his way through the undercity, keeping to the shadows. His black, hooded robe pulled tight over his face, concealing his identity. Although time was short, he kept a steady pace so he didn't draw any unnecessary attention to himself. He blended in with the other citizens of the Undercity in this section—the Dregs section. It was always dark here, with no sunlight in the slums. Over half of the lights were broken, making it easy for people like him to keep unnoticed, people like him and people like those searching for him. He knew it was only a matter of time before they found him, so he knew what he had to do.

It was dangerous in this part of the Undercity—as if any part of the Undercity was not dangerous—but this part, the Dregs as they called it, was almost deadly—indeed, it WAS deadly if you didn't know how to handle yourself here. The Dregs was full of the worst of the worst that dwelt in the undercity—not "lived" in the Undercity. To "live" meant to be more than surviving, and no one did anything in the Undercity but survive. Food was scarce, rationed by those living on the surface, those with all the power. While the populations grew down in the Dregs especially and in the Undercity, rarely did the top dwellers increase the rations, so food, sometimes, became a commodity worth killing over—especially in the Dregs.

The streets—especially the dark alleyways—were littered with the homeless and murderers lying in wait to prey upon the weak. The weak here, though, were not so soft. The Dregs of the Undercity was where the top dwellers brought their criminals. A dangerous place where food was worth more than a life and danger was the way of life. A place where plenty was rare and poverty was rampant. A place where perversions of every conceivable imagination kept those surviving in the Underdark from slipping away into the oblivion where hope, never attainable, was dreamt of in perverse pleasures.

That was why he chose this place, the Dregs, the darkest of the dark, the worst of the Undercity, the slums of the forgotten. He knew it wouldn't be long now before they discovered him, that he was missing. He had to make it there before they could find him. Every moment was another moment closer to certain death or victory, and he wouldn't allow himself death until he accomplished his task.

He slid from shadow to shadow, keeping clear of those huddled near the lights and keeping especially clear of those gathered around makeshift fires.

Scattered throughout the streets several hundred yards apart stood barrels filled with trash where men, women, and even children stood, huddled for warmth sometimes, but mostly for food. The fire pits, as they were called, were controlled by the gangs. Gangs created out of necessity more than anything else. Necessity for protection and food. Marked with gang signs so all knew that they belonged to the gangs, only the gang members were permitted to use the fire pits.

Some were smaller gangs and others were larger. The larger gangs kept the peace in the Dregs as they were feared. They killed those that broke their rules and killed those of other gangs caught in their territory, and it was even rumored that some of the smaller gangs even cannibalized enemy gangs.

Those huddled around lightposts not members of the gangs had to fend for themselves, gathering leftovers that the gangs left or scavenging for rodents and other creatures that made their homes among the Dregs.

The light was never bright, and sometimes, more light emanated from the fires than the dim street lights.

The gangs had their benefits, but the cost of membership was too high for some.

Membership always required some type of bodily mutilation, usually on the face—an identification to all of where you belonged or who one belonged to.

For the men, it was an easier initiation, but for the women, it wasn't as beneficial. The women were treated more like property here in the Dregs than humans, and as a gang member, their "womanly" duties were less than desirable.

No member could leave the boundaries of their territories for any reason, or they would be killed by rival gangs or their own gang for breaking the gang's law.

There was only one punishment for breaking the law of one's gang, no matter how small or big the crime—death.

Although those not aligned with a gang could venture anywhere in the Undercity and were relatively free from harm from most gangs, they too had to sacrifice. They did not reap the benefits of the protection and better food, and they had to fend for themselves in every aspect of their lives, from food to shelter to health.

The dwellings in the Dregs were first given to the gangs. If there were vacant buildings or rooms left after, then the "citizens" could use them. Until a gang member wanted it, at least.

Often, those not in a gang found a dark corner to hide and sleep, hoping that they would not be found and robbed or killed.

The hooded figure made sure to glance down the alleys as he passed, scanning them for any signs of danger. He saw, then, a half dozen peacekeepers. They dropped from the ceiling above, past the darkness. They came fast, and he knew what they came for.

They came to stop him.

He saw their lights before he saw them, and he knew it was them before they ever came close. They were the only ones who had such powerful lights. They were the only ones who had anything worth having. They were the peacekeepers, but they never kept the peace. When they came, it was death and violence that they brought, not peace, and they annihilated those who stood in the way or happened upon them at the wrong moment.

He knew time was running out. He could feel it within himself, and he saw it all around him.

There was only one reason the peacekeepers would be sent down to the Dregs like this. He was the reason.

He had to hurry.

***

He started walking faster now, faster than he should have—he knew—he had to risk it if he was going to complete his task.

He could sense now that he was being noticed as he rushed along the shadows with his hood up and face hidden, the shadows a welcome camouflage in the dark Dregs.

***

The soldiers were now boots on and quickly unlatched themselves from their ziplines, which shot back up into the darkness as they began searching for him. They moved fast, shining their lights into the faces of the citizens of the Underdark. Occasionally, a brave—or stupid—soul decided to attack one of the soldiers, hoping to overpower him and gain his weapon to attempt an escape back to the surface. It never ended well for the assailant. The soldiers were highly skilled in combat, both melee and ranged, the attacker never a match for them.

***

He started running now, the soldiers all behind him. He didn't have long to go, only a few more blocks, and he would be there. It would be a full crowd, and he knew if he could only make it there, then he could lose the soldiers, at least long enough to do what he knew he had to do.

Suddenly, two figures jumped into his path.

"You're the one they are after, aren't you?" one of them said.

Although he could hear the menace in the man's voice and sense the hostility in both, he didn't reply, he just kept going. He tried a quick maneuver around them, but the two anticipated this and maneuvered themselves again to block.

He didn't have time to waste and so advanced in full force—his attackers unaware of who they were about to engage.

The first of his attackers brought an arm up to stiff-arm the hooded figure. He immediately regretted it as excruciating pain erupted from his elbow, and he heard a crack then found his own fist in his face. His counterpart attempted a strike of his own with a makeshift knife fashioned out of a piece of thin metal. The next thing he knew, his own knife stuck painfully in his own leg, and the hooded figure's elbow was in his face.

Both men fell to the ground.

The hooded man now ran at full sprint, which caught the attention of the soldiers behind him. He could see the half-dozen light beams from their flashlights bouncing all around him. There was no doubt they saw him, he knew.

He rounded a corner and darted down the street. At this point, his running down the street attracted the attention of all those in the alleys and in the shadows themselves. Some attempted to stop him and ended up with a bloody nose or broken limb.

He soon rounded the next corner, the soldiers right behind. He rounded the corner into a large, crowded entertainment square. It spanned several blocks in every way and had an old, dried fountain in its center. Though there was no longer water flowing through the fountain, the gang that claimed this particular territory used it as a place to gather for entertainment for those that were of no gang affiliation.

The fountain was at least a city block wide with large stone blocks that stood anywhere from one story high to three stories scattered along the center of the square where, at one time, the blocks were used to direct the fountain's falls into one giant pool at the bottom. Now, it was used as a prostitution auction.

Atop every block stood women of all shapes and sizes, all of them wearing almost nothing, and a gang member stood on each side of them holding a thick chain that connected to a collar on the woman. Another chain attached from the collar to shackles, binding their hands.

The hooded figure glanced to his sides, scanning the square. To one side, he saw a makeshift ring made from barbed wire with a pair of armed combatants and a crowd cheering and hollering. To the other side, he saw makeshift rooms built out of scrap wood to which several gang members were escorting a man and one of their chained prostitutes into.

He darted toward the center of the square where the auction was being held, noticing as he dodged through the crowd several more gang members trading bags of powders, liquids, and leaves for various small bits of food and items.

As he scanned the courtyard, he noticed even more cages, rooms, drug dealers, and a few smaller groups engaging in hand-to-hand combat and other small groups gambling for items or women.

The soldiers rounded the corner soon after the hooded figure and immediately started searching for him in the crowd, shining their bright lights in the faces of those nearest them. Immediately, the occupants of the Undercity shuffled out of the way, not wanting to entice the wrath of the peacekeepers. The hooded figure stopped near the center of the square right in front of the prostitute auction and drew back his hood. He felt it now so intensely, and he released it.

His eyes began to shine a great, blinding light that pierced through the darkness.

The people around him each scurried out of the way, this sudden burst of light blinding them in the darkness. He opened his mouth then, and bright white light burst out again, breaking through the blackness of the Undercity.

The man looked inhuman as the beams of light poured from him.

The soldiers found him at this point, the beams of light emanating from him, a beacon. They flanked him, their weapons raised.

"Cease and desist," ordered one of the soldiers.

The square was now even more crowded with people as curious eyes ventured to the source of the chaos. They all stood back several yards, wanting nothing to do with the light nor the bullets that they knew would soon fly.

The robed man with glowing eyes moved slowly now as the soldiers aimed their deadly weapons, ordering him to stop what he knew he never could. He knew he couldn't, and he didn't want to. He had to show those down here the light that he had seen, and so he did what he knew he must.

He let his robe fall to the ground, revealing a bare chest tattooed with a black cross in the center.

The soldiers readied their weapons, unsure why the man dropped his cloak.

The cross on his chest began to glow dimly, growing brighter with every second. The man slowly lifted his arms above his head, the light emanating from the cross tattoo on his chest glowing even more brightly. Then with a sudden swing of his arms down, the glowing cross erupted into a brilliant flash of light blinding all those around him.

The last thing he heard were the soldier's screams before they fired. He had accomplished his task.

***

The lead peacekeeper stepped forward as the bare-chested man lay on the courtyard, blood seeping from the dozen holes in his chest.

The glow in the man's eyes, mouth, and glowing cross on his chest diminishing.

He knew this man lying before him. He had called him friend once. A fellow peacekeeper. He looked at his friend's lifeless body, and it was then as he thought of his friend and his pointless sacrifice in trying to show this "light" to these lowlifes that he sensed that something had changed in him. He couldn't put a finger on it exactly, maybe it was just the fact that he had killed a friend. Maybe it was something else.

He shoved his feelings and thoughts to the side.

"Mission accomplished. Let's go home," he said and turned, escorting his peacekeeper troops back through the Undercity.

***

She stood atop the tallest of the fountain blocks, the bright light vanishing just as quickly as it had erupted, but something was different. She didn't know what it was, but she knew she was different. She was the same, she knew, but she wasn't the same.

She looked around, and for the first time since she could remember, she was happy. She looked at all of the people in the square, and a smile grew on her face. She hadn't smiled in years.

She felt a pull on her neck and remembered where she was, what she was. It didn't matter. She felt free for the first time in her life, and no circumstance could take that freedom from her. She knew she would always be free, though she might be shackled now.

She looked down and saw the man she was just rented to, and still, her smile didn't fade. No matter what he or anyone else did to her body, she was free now somehow.

Somehow, that light had changed her forever.

***

He opened his eyes, almost slipping off the edge of the short fountain block he stood on. He blinked several times, blinking the spots out of his eyes from the flash of blinding light.

He looked over to the woman by his side, a new girl. He knew that she was forced into this prostitution because she couldn't pay back what the gang had loaned her mother. She was sixteen, and her mother had died only months ago, but her mother had debt, and debt always transferred to the children—if one was unfortunate enough to have children in this place.

Something happened to him that he didn't expect when he looked into her eyes. He could see the fear in her eyes. He could see the shame on her face. For the first time in his life, he wanted to help. He was a criminal in the city, and he quickly made a name for himself in his gang when he was sent to the Undercity, but now, he wasn't sure what was happening to him. He had never before cared about another person other than himself, and now, compassion for this young girl overwhelmed him, and he began to cry. Only a few tears, and he wiped them before anyone else could see. Anyone else except the sixteen-year-old next to him. When she turned, he grabbed her by the neck. Not rough like he used to, but gently, and he felt even worse for this girl as she flinched when he touched her. Before, when he grabbed her neck, a fist always followed. He didn't hit her this time. Instead, he released the pin holding her collar in place and then released her wrist shackles.

He knew he was signing his death certificate by letting her go, but he didn't care. Something had changed in him after seeing the light.

"Go, run," he whispered to the girl as she stared at him in astonishment. The girl flung off her wrist shackles and tossed her collar aside then darted away as her savior stepped behind the girl and pushed the other off of the short block.

He waited until the girl disappeared into the crowd before jumping off the block, knocking as many of his fellow gang members down as he could.

He fled the opposite way.

***

The cage fighter peered through the barbed wire fence out toward where the light had come from. He ignored his opponent who was recovering as well from the blinding flash of light. It had all happened so fast; at first, he didn't know what had happened, but as he watched, when his eyes re-focused, he understood. Someone had shown the light that came from within themselves and was killed for it. Why? He couldn't say. Why here? He couldn't imagine.

All he knew now was that it had forever changed him.

He didn't understand it, but he wanted more of that light.

The man suddenly felt a sharp pain in his back and cold steel sink deep into the small of his back as his opponent took advantage of the distraction. Then, he felt it slide out. Then another sharp pain. Again, it slid out. Again and again and again he felt the cold steel pierce his skin and slide out.

He fell to his knees, spitting blood, then as he fell onto his face, he smiled. He had been changed by the light, and he wanted more light. Now, somehow, he knew he was going to be with the light and see the light in mere moments.

Dothan

Gahazi woke up early and donned a tunic and leggings, strapping a belt around his waist over both his leggings and tunic to keep his leggings up and his tunic from flapping in the wind.

He rinsed his face in a washbasin he'd prepared the night before. The cold water helped to wake him up in the mornings.

After splashing the cold water on his face, he slipped into his sandals and snatched his satchel up, along with a bag of coins, and headed out the door, noticing that Elisha was already awake and working on his model.

They ignored each other as Elisha focused intently on his model and Gahazi crossed the room, setting out for his morning duties.

As Gahazi's morning ritual was to venture to the city market, it was Elisha's morning ritual to work on his models. It relaxed him, calmed him, and focused his mind.

He had been making models for years; his current model was of the outside of the Israelite temple. Now, he was adding the outer court.

He had hand carved each and every piece to his model, and now, he was gluing them together with a concoction made from warm tree sap mixed with a few other compounds found in nature.

He dipped a carved piece into the heated sap and slowly, gently, tucked it into its predetermined place.

He was so engrossed in his creation that he barely noticed his servant cross the room and shut the door.

****

Gahazi busied himself with buying the daily and weekly supplies.

The market was conveniently just around the corner from the house, so it made the trip to the market a fast and easy morning task.

Once he found everything he needed in the central market, he ventured further toward the outskirts of the small town of Dothan, where the last of the merchant stands stood.

He always enjoyed shopping for supplies along the outskirts of the market because the city opened up into a large, clear plot of land that had no houses or shops to block the view of the surrounding mountains or valley. He would always take a few minutes to enjoy the view. Though Dothan was small, it had many buildings that stood tall, even a few two-story shops that blocked the view of the surrounding valley and mountains, except in the one spot where the market snaked out to.

His morning shopping was cut short when he noticed several shoppers start panicking, and he, himself, began panicking as he looked out over the open field to see an army surrounding the city. Hundreds of horses and chariots and armed foot soldiers stood a mere hundred yards away.

He dropped the few things that he had not stuffed in his satchel and raced home.

***

Elisha was just about to set another delicate piece into his model when Gahazi threw open the door.

"Master!" he yelled, running into his bedroom. "We have to go!"

Gahazi dropped the contents of his satchel onto his bed and began stuffing clothes into it.

"Master! Hurry!" he ordered and darted out of his bedroom.

He paused as he saw Elisha calmly sitting before his model dipping another fragile piece into his homemade glue and setting it into its predestined place.

"What are you doing?" Gahazi asked as he rushed over to a wall of cupboards. "We have got to go! We are about to be attacked!" Gahazi shoved several bread rolls and fruits into his satchel.

"I know," Elisha replied softly as he dipped another piece and inserted it into the proper place in his model. "We will be fine."

"Fine! Fine! There is an army ready to attack. How will we be fine?" Gahazi yelled. "What shall we do?"

"Don't be afraid. Those who are with us are more than those who are with them," Elisha replied, scrutinizing his model intently for anything he might have missed then stood.

"Come with me."

"What, where?" Elisha ignored the question as he left the house.

Gahazi followed Elisha around the corner and through the market. They had to dodge townspeople frantically running through the town, searching for loved ones, bumping and crashing into each other in panic. Some shoved their way through the small merchant tables to try to bypass the shoving crowds, and others altogether turned over merchant tables, knocking their contents to the ground without regard as they fled. Some even looted food and clothing as they ran, and even the merchants in the market left their merchandise and fled, hoping to find safety before the army attacked.

"Master, where are we going? The army is that way!" Gahazi exclaimed. Elisha ignored him.

Elisha finally stopped as they reached the outskirts of the city. Gahazi moved around him and began heading into the trees, hoping to take shelter somewhere that the army would not find him.

"Gahazi," Elisha said. "Stop."

Gahazi stopped and turned, confused.

"Come here," Elisha ordered.

Gahazi couldn't understand how his master could be so calm. He could even hear the calmness in Elisha's voice. He spoke as if he were merely watching the sunset or children playing. *Not* as if he were staring at an army about to attack.

"Gahazi, come here; I want to show you something."

"Can't this wait until we are safe?"

Elisha stared at Gahazi, waiting for Gahazi to return to his side.

"We are in no danger," Elisha explained, seeing the fear on Gahazi's face and closed his eyes.

"Open his eyes LORD so that he may see," Elisha whispered.

Gahazi fell to his knees gasping for breath. He had heard his master pray for his eyes to be opened, and what he saw struck even more fear into his heart than the enemy army surrounding them. He couldn't move. Fear gripped him so tightly that he could barely breathe. He tried to speak, but fear's paralyzing grasp squeezed his throat so tightly that only a whisper escaped, and his mouth had become so dry that he couldn't even force more than a syllable out.

Gahazi had never felt fear so powerful, had never thought fear *could* even do such things to him.

He couldn't even close his eyes or cry out in terror. Every muscle in his body tensed so tightly that he felt like he was a statue—frozen.

All he could do was stare at the massive army that appeared before him. At the horses that breathed fire from their noses. Horses twice the size of those of the enemy army. The bright flames puffed from their nostrils, lighting up their glossy white coats, and their riders were massive creatures that seemed to emanate light. They too were twice as large as any man Gahazi had ever seen.

Chariots of pure white sat behind even more horses, horses that were larger than those with riders, and the occupants of the chariots larger than the riders as well. The chariot wheels looked as if they were flames. Not wheels with flames, but the flames themselves *were* the wheels.

"Those who are with us are more than those who are with them," Elisha said.

Gahazi looked out over the vast open landscape to see standing between them and the enemy army hundreds of these massive, giant creatures. He saw even behind this enemy army the great and massive army of white and fire spanning for as far as he could see.

Then, in unison, they all drew their swords. The ringing was so loud that Gahazi had to bring his hands up to his ears to shield his eardrums.

Then all was silent. Gahazi looked up and saw only the enemy army. They seemed small now and non-threatening. Gahazi understood now. They were in no danger.

He sat against a tree stump and waited calmly with Elisha to see what would happen to this little army.

The Touch

Two men walked down a suburban street around noon. The first, a tall, slender man, and the second a short, stalky fellow.

"Wait," said the short stalky fellow. "Can you change that car?" he asked, pointing to an old '57 Chevy with rusted, sun-bleached paint and riddled with holes from the corroding metal. It had several windows that were shattered, with a portion of the window still attached near the bottom. It had one door primer gray and the hood had been sanded down, bare of paint. Its owner was in the beginning processes of fixing it up.

"Just watch," the tall, slender man replied and walked over to the once beautiful car. He slid his fingertips along the car's hood as he walked by its front then continued sliding his hand up the cracked windshield and onto the roof of the vehicle.

The short, stalky fellow's jaw dropped at what he saw. The instant the tall man touched the hood, the car began to morph. It seemed as if the car painted itself. Where the man touched, the primer gray turned a bright red and spread out along the hood until the color covered it entirely. As the man passed his fingers up the cracked windshield, the crack vanished, leaving the windshield sparkling like new.

The tall man continued his walk to the rear of the car, sliding his hand along the roof, down the rear window, and finally, off the back of the Chevy. The entire time, the once sun-bleached paint miraculously turned a bright red, and the rusted holes closed themselves up, disappearing before the paint covered them bright red. The broken out windows grew out from the edges of the window frames, and the newer side door painted itself bright red.

"Like new," the tall man said as he finished.

"Whoa, it's like totally new!" the short fellow replied.

"Indeed."

"That's so cool," the stalky fellow exclaimed in amazement.

He noticed a small, dead bush then, its leaves dry and crinkly.

"What about this?" he asked as he rushed over to the bush. "Can you make it come alive?"

The tall, slender man walked over to the small, dead bush and knelt beside it. He gently took a dead branch, lifting it gingerly as he hunched closer to the fragile plant and lightly blew on the tip of the branch resting in his palm. The short, stalky fellow gasped at what he saw.

The brown, decaying leaves at the tip of the branch his friend was holding began to change color. Slowly, the brown brightened into a deep green from the very tip of the last leaf. The color, as if someone were painting, grew out, engulfing the entire leaf in the new green. From there, it spread to its surrounding leaves, and then their surrounding leaves, and so on and so forth. It cascaded out over the entire bush, spreading as if a wildfire had engulfed it.

As the green filled more and more of it, the branches themselves seemed to gain strength and lift themselves up from their wilting, straight out, reaching toward the sky. It was as if

the bush was waking up and stretching. Seconds later, the green

had thoroughly colored the whole of the plant, and as it

completed the color transformation, the outermost branches

began to sprout beautiful roses. These roses, however, were no

ordinary roses. They did not grow in just one color, as other rose

bushes did, but the bush sprouted roses of various colors and

fades. Red, yellow, blue, green, white, pink, even multicolored

combinations such as blue-green, white-red, red-yellow, blue-

white, pink-green, white-black, and more. It now contained an

array of the most magnificent roses in every variation

imaginable.

The short, stalky fellow knew this once dead organism

would forever be changed by the touch of his friend—the

resurrecting breath of his friend. He stood in amazement for a

few more seconds in awe of the beauty then scanned the street

for more broken or rundown items for his friend to make new or

come alive.

He saw a field of dry, dead, brown grass and his eyes lit
up.

"What about that?" he asked.

The tall man, standing at this point, nodded.

"Come on, then; let's see it!" he exclaimed as he hurried
across the street. The tall man rushed to catch up to him. When
they reached the edge of the field, the stalky fellow looked at his
friend expectantly. The tall man smiled at his short friend,
turned to face the field and waved a hand out toward the field.

The dry, brittle grass at their feet instantly transformed
into soft, rich, green, healthy grass. The weeds at their feet
morphed into flowers. The new green grass at their feet spread
out in a wave like a tsunami devouring the ocean before it. The
fresh, healthy green grass rolling out into the field, seeming to
consume the dry, dead grass, the weeds strewn throughout the
field changing into various flowers of all sorts, leaving the dark
green of the grass sprayed with a rainbow of color. Again, the
stalky fellow gasped in awe.

It was then that the tall man turned to the short, stalky fellow with his arms wide and his palms out. He reached out to touch the short fellow, but he stepped back several feet.

"What are you doing?" the short, stalky fellow asked, frightened.

"It's your turn." The tall man opened his arms out toward him.

"No, no, I'm okay just the way I am," the short man said, taking several more steps backward.

***

We all so often enjoy watching others get changed, but seldom do we acknowledge the fact that we need to be changed—or even want to change, even if it's for the better.

***

Burdens

A lone traveler wearily inched his way across the long, hot desert, his clothes soaked with sweat, and his skin coated with grime and dirt. He could feel his dirty sweat trickle down his arms and drip off of his elbows as he carried his burdens over his shoulders, keeping a strong but weary hold of them, ensuring that they did not fall. They were delicate and heavy, yet he did not know why he carried them. All he knew was that he was to carry them. He held one draped over each shoulder; one was a bundle of sticks tied together with tiny, fraying rope. The other was a three-foot-long, thin mirror that he balanced on his dirty and sweaty shoulder.

"I got to keep going," he mumbled to himself, more for self-motivation than anything else. He kept his eyes low, right on the desert floor in front of him. He feared that if he moved his head too much that he would lose the balance of his burdens, so he stared at nothing but the ground right in front of him.

"I got to make it," he said.

***

A man stood on a balance with a noose around his neck, watching the lone traveler off in the distance, his legs spread wide, one foot on each side of the balance arms. His hands were tied around his waist so he couldn't use them for balance, let alone to free himself. His legs burned like fire, and every muscle in his body ached. He had been balancing himself for who knows how long that day. It felt like hours, though he knew it was just minutes. He knew that he couldn't keep balancing on this torture device much longer. His legs shook with weariness. He shifted his weight slightly onto one leg to give the other a slight rest, and then shifted his weight to the other leg. It didn't help. He tried resting his legs just enough to where the noose held him up only slightly, but the choking was unbearable.

Sweat dripped from him like a leaking faucet, and despair began to fill him. There was no way he would be able to get out of this—he would die in this barren land.

***

The lone traveler suddenly felt a reprieve from the scorching heat as a cloud shaded the sky above him, and he sighed in thankful relief. The lack of skin-scorching rays brought a measure of rejuvenation to his steps, and he walked just a little faster, his burdens seeming just a little bit lighter.

"I got to make it," he said louder now. He didn't really know why he felt so strongly that he had to make it. He could just give up and go back where he came from or just drop his burdens and go somewhere else, somewhere other than where he was supposed to go, somewhere that would be easier to get to. He knew, though, that if he didn't make it, something terrible would happen, so he knew that he had to make it.

The cloud passed by, and the sun brought a new wave of scorching rays. Rays that seemed to burn even worse than before. His steps almost immediately became shuffles as his trial seemed to worsen. Indeed, his trial did worsen. He hadn't noticed it before, looking down at the ground, or maybe none of them were in his sight. Either way, he noticed them now, snake holes along his path; not just any snake holes, he quickly

discovered, but rattlesnake holes. He heard them behind him.
He didn't notice them at first, but as he passed by a few holes, he
noticed them start to slither out of their holes. He heard at first
an almost unnoticeable rattle, then it grew louder and louder. He
knew that it grew louder because more and more were following
him.

He picked up his pace, keeping as steady as possible as
to not drop his burdens. Burdens that he knew he needed to
carry. He dared not look back, both for fear of the threat that he
would see, as well as not wanting to chance too much movement
and drop his burdens.

***

The man balanced on the balance, his legs on fire and his
body sore from tension. He watched the lone traveler getting
closer. He was close enough, now, to see that the traveler kept
his head down. He was close enough to see the dark forms
gathering behind him, following him. At first, he couldn't make
out what the mysterious forms were, but as they neared, he
finally realized they were snakes. He tried to yell to warn the

traveler, but as he hollered, nothing came out; his throat was so dry, and he stopped short anyway as his attempt at yelling unbalanced him slightly, and he had to quickly recover before he fell and hung himself.

He watched now in total and utter despair, knowing that even if he tried to call out, he wouldn't be able to, nor would he survive the attempt. He watched the man closely now. The snakes behind him a black stain on the brown desert floor. He feared, now, for the man's survival, knowing full well that his own survival was not possible. At least he could get some semblance of solace at his death if he were able to stay alive long enough to see this man overcome his trial—at least until he was out of sight. Then he would give up and allow the noose around his neck to kill him.

***

The lone traveler ignored the rattling of the snakes behind him. He walked as fast as he could without dropping his burdens and was thankful when he heard the rattling stop. He assumed they stopped chasing him but dared not look back. He passed by a shadow then. Thankful for another cloud, he

glanced into the long, thin mirror to see how big the cloud might

be and how long he might have shade and gasped as he saw a

man staring down at him. He froze, the man's reflection in his

mirror.

***

The man watched the traveler passing by, unable to

speak, but thankful that he had survived the snakes. He wished

he could do something, anything to ask for help, but he couldn't.

Then he saw the man freeze. He saw the man staring at him in

the mirror he carried.

***

The lone traveler suddenly realized why he had picked

up these burdens along his journey. He dropped the mirror,

hearing it shatter but suddenly didn't care. He turned and looked

up, grabbing the pile of sticks in both hands.

***

As he balanced on the balance, looking down on the lone traveler, despair fled and hope rushed in. The traveler dropped his mirror and turned to him. He set a bundle of sticks on the ground under one of the sides of the balance, removing one stick from the bundle, and wedged it under the balance.

***

The lone traveler secured one side of the balance.

"Try not to move, but keep your balance as best you can," he said, making sure the bundle was secure then took the single stick holding it by its end and reached up. He caught the noose in a tiny crevice the on the tip of the stick and lifted the noose off of the man's neck.

***

The man watched as this stranger removed the noose, then he fell limp. He fell hard to the desert floor but didn't care. His heart was filled with complete and total joy at being free.

The stranger rushed over to the man, handing him a water skin, then realized his hands were tied to his waist and rushed over to the broken mirror, snatched up a shard, and cut the rope binding the man.

The man snatched the water skin and guzzled. After he had his fill, he returned the empty water skin with an apologetic grin.

"Thank you," he said with a hoarse voice. "I didn't think you were going to see me."

"I almost didn't; I thought your shadow was a cloud."

The man nodded.

"I owe you my life."

"Nonsense, I was supposed to walk this path and find you; I know that now."

The man nodded again.

"There is a well not far along the way you were headed. You can replenish your water there. I feel I must journey with you."

The traveler nodded.

"If you feel you must, but it is not necessary or expected."

"I do."

"Well then, let's get that water." The traveler stood up and held out a hand to help the other up.

***

They reached the well, filled their waterskin, and as they turned to leave, they noticed a thick rope net filled with small boulders. The traveler's new friend paused.

"What is it," he asked.

"I feel like we need to take that."

"Then we shall. I have learned that we always have a reason we carry our burdens."

The man nodded and picked up the heavy burden.

"I will help you until I find my own burdens to carry," the traveler said, and the duo carried the load together.

***

Off in the distance, beyond sight, stood a woman on a balance.

***

As believers, we have to keep going because someone else's life may hang in the balance.

***

Bonus Story

The King's Daughter Part 1: Labyrinth

Shiela and Grawn stood before the great labyrinth. It was a massive structure made of thick, magical hedges. Looming in the distance stood the high tower that was their destination.

The clouds hung low amid the sculpted brush, and the tower seemed almost as if it were a part of the fog around it. They both could see the winged creatures circling the tower, and they both knew that monstrosities of all kinds waited in that labyrinth. But they had ventured this far already, and they had a quest to complete. Their companions had been killed on their long journey already, and they had long to go still.

They each had vowed that they would fulfill the quest or die trying, and indeed, all but the two of them had fulfilled their vow.

"Are you ready?" Grawn asked. He was a massive man, standing six feet tall, and his bulging muscles made any man think twice before challenging him. He wore leggings and thick leather boots, and his bare, chiseled, rockhard torso made any woman's eyes linger.

Shiela nodded in reply, and the two began their journey into the labyrinth.

Dwarfed by her enormous counterpart, Shiela stood in the lower end of five feet. Her long hair blew lightly in the wind, and her petite figure deceptively lent to her opponent's gravely underestimating her. Her loose-fitting leggings and cloak flapping in the breeze gave a disarming sense of innocence to her foes.

The two cautiously made their way through the threshold of the labyrinth noticing the surrounding fog seem to react to their very presence, swirling and twisting outward away from them. Then a high-pitched squeal echoed throughout the maze with such shrill coldness that it sent shivers down the battle-hardened warriors. The labyrinth walls themselves twisted and shifted, scraping eerily against each other.

Shiela tightened her grip on her bow, and Grawn squeezed the handle of his heavy, two-edged axe, both pausing as they scanned their surroundings.

They felt the danger now. It seemed to ride the wind and seep into their skin, morphing into fear as it flowed into the core of their beings.

Neither dared to speak for fear that even a whisper would awaken some monstrous evil. They had expected this. They were warned that an unnatural fear would overwhelm them, but they had not believed the magnitude of the sensation washing over them.

Then everything went silent. The shrill shriek stopped, and the walls of the labyrinth froze. The only movement was the fog swirling and shifting along the path in front of them.

"We must continue," Grawn said with a shaky voice. It was more for himself than it was for Shiela.

His deep voice cut through the deafening silence with such force that the sudden disruption made Shiela cringe as if he had yelled right into her ear.

She nodded and took a step, Grawn following her lead. It seemed for the both of them that the moment their feet landed the step their fear diminished slightly. Each step after that first was just a little easier until the fear had been completely pushed to the back of their minds. It no longer debilitated them but strengthened them. It made them more alert. Every sound echoed in their ears, and every movement caught their eyes.

They walked on, and the unnatural fear leaked away with every new step.

They soon found themselves at an intersection and paused.

Peering down both passages, they saw nothing but darkness. Even the hedges vanished into blackness as they stretched on.

"I think it's time to use the magic sphere," Shiela said quietly, not wanting to disturb the quiet stillness.

Grawn nodded and pulled a small, white, marble sphere from a pocket in his leggings. The orb, like everything in his hands, seemed tiny in his palm. He cupped the marble in his hand, allowing it to roll back and forth, then lifted his palm to his mouth.

"Take us to the tower," he spoke into his palm and then blew a heavy breath onto the marble.

The marble instantly began vibrating and rose to eye level with Grawn, who stood motionless, his eyes wide.

The white marble began humming and glowing white so brightly against the blackness of the night that Grawn had to step back and bring a hand up to shield himself from the blinding light.

Though Shiela was not as close, she too had to shield her eyes from the magic orb.

The glowing ball floated backward a few feet then moved down the left hedge trail. The two followed the guiding light down the path and around several bends, half a dozen forked passages, and several three-way splits.

The floating orb kept several feet ahead, pausing around bends until the two founded the corner then moved forward again.

They finally came to a chamber in the hedge maze, and again, a fresh wave of terror flooded through them.

They froze, all of their senses heightened in fear once again. They scanned the chamber seeing nothing stirring in the large open square. No obstacles to hinder their crossing, no enemies to block their way. Nothing. It was a simple, empty square spanning thirty feet both in length and width. The glowing orb halted at the center of the chamber, shot upward several feet above the maze hedges, and started frantically pulsing even brighter, lighting up the square even more with a pulsating strobe effect.

The two heroes stood in crippling horror as the strobe lighting revealed three bat-like creatures atop the hedges each straddling an exit in the center of each wall.

They stared in terror as the three creatures glared back at them. The creatures weren't moving, merely staring, and after several long moments, Grawn took a step.

He cringed as his boot thumped onto the stone flooring, the utter silence seeming to magnify the sound.

It was the first time he noticed that the labyrinth flooring was that of stone. As quickly as he noticed, though, he forgot about it, returning his gaze back up and glancing back and forth among the three monstrosities atop the hedge walls.

It was then that he realized they were mere ornaments meant to strike fear into those who entered the chamber. And fear they did evoke.

"They are not real," he exclaimed as he took another step.

"Maybe not," Sheila replied as she took a few steps of her own, "but there is an evil here."

"I feel it too, just like when we first entered the labyrinth."

"An unnatural fear surrounds this place," Shiela added.

The two began walking to the center of the chamber beneath the orb.

"A tactic to keep the weak-willed away," Grawn said.

"Well, it's not made any better by our magic ball doing that." Shiela pointed up to the pulsating sphere.

Suddenly, the bat-like creature straddling the entryway in front of them burst into action. It launched forward, fluttering its wings so fast and violently that a cloud of dust shot into the air from the stone floor, and within seconds, the chamber went dark as the beast engulfed the tiny glowing sphere whole.

Shiela and Grawn tumbled to their backs as the creature startled them, devouring their only means to see the beast.

Untamed fear gripped them once again, and they frantically jumped to their feet, hearing the swishing of more fluttering wings and smelling the choking clouds of dust unsettled by the powerful creatures. They both swung their weapons blindly toward the sounds of their unseen monstrous foes. With every second that passed, their fear grew, and they spun more frantically, swinging their weapons out in panicked defense.

Finally, their eyes began to adjust to the dim moonlight, a mere sliver compared to the glowing sphere, but it allowed them to see their foe, and they almost wished they couldn't see the monstrosities before them.

The three bat-like creatures stood tall on their hind legs at eye level with Grawn. Their wings were tucked in, wrapping around their abdomens and long arms that ended in three claws. Their faces looked as if they were a combination of bat and bird with a long, fat, fleshy beak that ended in a bat-like nose and rows of sharp teeth that stretched all the way to the back of their beaks. The beasts' eyes were that of bat eyes, and their ears were pointed as bat's ears were.

They were green and looked as if they were both plant and demon spawn. Their flesh was a mixture of leaf-like scales that matched the hedge plants, and their veins protruded between their scales, resembling twigs and branches.

The three beasts screeched a high, ear-piercing cry, revealing their deadly teeth even more, and the two heroes felt a fresh wave of total and utter terror rush through them.

The two heroes stood staring at the three creatures before them, their hearts pounding in their chests. All they wanted to do was flee, but they knew the moment they turned their backs to the creatures they were dead.

Neither had ever run from a battle, and neither had ever even considered it until now, and they both knew that it was due to the unnatural terror swelling within them.

They fought with every ounce of willpower to keep calm, forcing the fear down as deep as they could, knowing that if they released their grip on the fear in the slightest, it would overtake and consume them.

The three bat-like beasts spread out, flanking them.

The two heroes turned with the flanking creatures, keeping their eyes on both the middle beast and their flanking foe.

Shiela slowly brought an arm up over her back, reaching for an arrow from the quiver strapped to her back. The quiver protruded out of a slot in her cloak at her left shoulder, specifically cut from the cloak for easy and quick access to her deadly weapons.

She didn't want to move too quickly, startling or angering the fierce creatures into attacking.

Grawn tightened his grip on his double-bladed, heavy axe and brought his axe blade up chest level, readying for a swing.

Suddenly, the middle beast gurgled a deep screech, catching the attention of the two flanking fiendish birds and sending another wave of fear through the heroes.

Grawn and Shiela both shuffled back several steps, and the two flanking birds jumped backward with a frightened shriek of their own.

The middle bird stumbled backward several steps as it let out several more low, gurgled screeches. Its stomach began glowing an orangish red, and the bat-like bird began flapping its massive wings frantically, gurgling more screeches.

The winged monster flew up a few feet, startling its flanking counterparts, which shuffled backward several steps.

The airborne monster gurgled another low screech and fell to the labyrinth stone with a thud and began writhing, its abdomen glowing brighter and finally bursting into flames.

The creature fell silent and still as the tiny, white, glowing orb burst out of the monster's flaming stomach and shot back up into the center of the chamber, lighting the square.

The two flanking bat-like monsters shrieked an angry ear-piercing scream and burst into action.

The closest to Grawn lunged at him, who luckily had already maneuvered his axe between them, saving his life as the bird-like beast, lightning fast, sent a deadly beak toward Grawn's face.

Grawn barely dodged the almost-fatal peck, leaning sideways as he hefted his battle axe up to block the ferocious creature.

The heavy axe lurched upward into the beast's beak, forcing the massive monster's head upward as Grawn leaned.

The deadly, pointed beak with its razor-sharp teeth missed its mark, but not before leaving a stinging gash across Grawn's cheek.

Grawn stumbled sideways as the huge beast clumsily stumbled forward and plowed into him, momentarily caught off balance from the jar to its beak.

Seconds later, the deadly bat creature was upon him with a fierceness that frightened even him. It sent a constant barrage of pecks toward him while slashing at him with its deadly claws.

Grawn parried and blocked, parried and blocked, parried and blocked over and over again, each slash or peck getting that much closer to landing its blow.

****

Shiela dove to the hard labyrinth stone as her opponent sprung into flight with one powerful beat of its wings, shooting forward at her like an arrow.

Nocking the arrow she had pulled from her quiver as she dove, Shiela rolled out of her dive onto one knee and sent it flying.

The arrow hit its mark, sinking deep into the green creature's torso as it landed and spun for a second attack. The green-scaled, bird-like monster screeched in pain and anger and charged.

The second she loosed her arrow, she reached for another, nocking and loosing it with the swiftness and accuracy of a master bowman, then rolled just as the bat-like monster reached her.

The arrow found its mark again, right next to her first, and she loosed two more arrows, which found their marks before she had to dodge again.

The arrows were having no effect on the bird, so she changed her aim.

***

Grawn now fought desperately to fend off the fierce attacks, and he feared that he would soon fulfill his vow. He was being pushed back, and he knew the hedge wall was nearing, but the green-scaled bat creature had countered every move he made to change course. He knew the bird was leading him to the wall to corner him.

He had an idea then. A dangerous idea and one that would likely end up with this monster's toothy beak plucking chunks of flesh from his corpse, but he could see no other alternative.

He opened himself up for a deadly attack, resting the flat of his blade on his shoulder and falling to his back as the bird-like bat creature slashed and pecked. To his luck, the green scaled bird was already in mid-peck before it realized Grawn's advantage.

The bird adjusted its attack the second it had realized Grawn had fallen to the ground but not before Grawn brought his heavy axe up into the creature's exposed belly. The bat-bird screeched in pain as Grawn's axe sunk deep into the scaly monster's flesh.

A stinging, itching flash of pain erupted across Grawn's chest from his left shoulder down to his right hip, and he felt the warmth of his blood against his skin.

***

Shiela rolled back to her feet, snatching another arrow from her quiver, and fired again, this time aiming for the green-scaled creature's knee. Without hesitation, she snatched another arrow and fired, then another, then another, and another in a matter of seconds.

The bat-bird monster barreled down on her with a ferocity and speed that sent a chill down her spine. Her heart beat heavier, and her stomach knotted more and more with every loosed arrow as the monster before her loomed closer and closer.

Arrow after arrow hit its mark, and the bird creature continued; then, finally, as the last arrow sank deep between the green scales, the monster tumbled right toward Shiela. Again, she dove to the side as the beast tumbled to the ground, its toothy beak passing inches from her feet as the monster snapped for her.

73

She rolled to her feet in one swift motion and released three more arrows into the bird's eye before the beast even had a chance to recover.

The bird went limp, and Shiela sighed in relief; then she heard the ear-piercing shriek of the other creature and suddenly remembered Grawn.

***

Grawn lifted the lifeless bird off of him, groaning in pain. Warm blood pooled around him, and a fresh, bloody gash that lay diagonally across his chest stung with such intensity that he feared the pool of blood was his. Then he saw his exe protruding from the bat-like bird and the blood gushing from its wound.

"Grawn!" Shiela said, rushing over upon seeing him lying in a pool of blood.

"I am alive," he replied and slowly crawled to his feet with a grimace. Every movement of his arms brought a fresh surge of pain through his chest.

"Are you alright?" Shiela asked with concern at seeing the gaping slash across Grawn's midsection.

"I will be fine," he replied as he yanked his axe out of the corpse.

The orb lowered to eye level and dimmed to its previous glow, allowing the darkness to swallow the courtyard into shadows and barely perceptible forms.

The two heroes froze as the darkness swept in and the paralyzing fear returned once more. Again, their senses heightened as the fear rushed in and they fought against panic.

After what seemed like hours, their eyes finally adjusted to the lower illumination of the guiding sphere.

"Come on," Grawn said finally and began toward the orb at the center of the courtyard, and the guiding light began moving toward the entryway to the right of the pathway they had entered the courtyard from.

"Hold on," Shiela said, and hurriedly retrieved her arrows, wiping them off on her cloak and returning them into her quiver. "Okay, let's go."

Shiela fell into step next to Grawn, and the two followed their magical guide.

***

Left, right, left, left, right, right, right, left, left, right, left, right, right. Left, then a three-way split and two more lefts and the labyrinth opened up into another chamber. The orb shot to the center of the courtyard and up again, exploding in light.

Shiela and Grawn, again blinded by the bright light, shielded their eyes and once again an unnatural terror engulfed them as they heard a deep, guttural grunt of surprise resounding through the chamber.

Shiela tightened her grip on her bowstring, and Grawn squeezed his double-axe blade handle so tightly that his knuckles turned white.

When their eyes grew accustomed again to the brightness, what they saw across the stone courtyard brought a terror into their hearts like they had yet to experience. In the back of their minds, they knew that the unnatural fear that pervaded this labyrinth had much to do with the fear that they both felt, but just the sight alone of this enormous monstrosity would strike fear into the most hardened of warriors.

Across the chamber stood a massive beast ten feet tall. It held no weapon, but that did not alleviate any dismay at the sight of this creature. Its bare torso was that of a human with bulging muscles, the arms of which were twice as big as Grawn's. Its legs were that of an ox, its hooves clattering on the stone floor as the beast moved. The two could tell even from across the chamber that its legs were strong and powerful, even through the knotted and matted clumps of long, thick, brown fur.

The most terrifying thing about this creature was not its powerful ox legs or its inhumanly massive, hairless body but its bull's head. A mane of thick, mangled, brown fur stretched down the beast's back, and its horns stretched out several feet in front of its massive bull's nose. Its furry head, like a helmet hung down past its neck, and though it had no weapon, both heroes knew this minotaur was indeed itself a weapon.

The minitour bellowed a deep growl and charged, and the two fought the urge to flee. The beast charged with its head low, and with an uncanny swiftness, it was upon them in mere seconds.

Shiela loosed two arrows before diving out of the way, which bounced harmlessly off of the minotaur's thick human hide, and Grawn brought his double-bladed axe up and out as he dove to the side, grazing the minotaur's immense arm.

The minotaur roared in anger as it sped past the two, skidding to a halt with its powerful hooved legs just before plowing into the thick hedge wall.

Shiela was back on her feet a second later, loosing two more arrows that again bounced off of her massive foe's thick hide.

The beast spun and charged again; again, Shiela dove out of the way, barely dodging a horn, but the creature's arm struck her hard in the calf, sending her spinning with a surge of fresh pain. She smacked painfully into the hard, cold stone floor, rolling clumsily until she finally stopped several feet from her foe.

She jumped to her feet as the massive monster barreled down on her once more, then she fell to the stone floor with a squeal as her calf surged with a fresh wave of pain and then gave out.

She had no time to move out of the way. She stared into the face of the minotaur as it barreled down on her, mere inches away, and suddenly the beast lurched sideways with a deep grunt and tumbled to the ground.

***

Grawn crawled to his feet as quickly as his large body would allow him. He was big and strong, which came in handy in brawls, but his size and strength came with its disadvantages. He was slow getting to his feet—at least slower than many.

When he finally did get to his feet, he saw the minitour racing toward Shiela as she dropped to the ground.

Without hesitation, he charged for the massive beast. Half a second before the monster reached Shiela, he plowed into the creature, and the two went tumbling to the ground.

Grawn rolled away from his foe and as quickly as he could scrambled to his feet. Thankfully, the minotaur, though fast with his charges, was not so quick in recovering. Grawn launched into an attack while the massive beast was still crawling to its hooves, bringing his heavy axe down into the creature's thigh.

The minotaur howled in pain and fell back to the stone floor as Grawn's axe sank deep into its leg.

Grawn yanked his axe out and brought his it up for another attack, but his foe rolled to the side, dodging Grawn's second attack. His axe blade clanged hard against the stone floor, jarring Grawn's arms painfully.

"Grawn!" Shiela hollered. "The exit!"

Grawn looked over at Shiela and glanced toward the direction she was pointing. He saw that in the alcove in which the minotaur had been standing when the two had entered stood another exit.

Shiela had already stood back to her feet and began limping her way to the exit.

Grawn immediately rushed to her side, wrapping an arm around her, helping her toward the alcove.

The minotaur stood to its feet and limped its way to the two heroes as well, gaining on them despite its injured leg.

A red light started glowing at the center of the alcove's hedge archway above the exit then flared into a blinding red light. Again, the two brought up a shielding hand.

Seconds later, their vision returned, and they saw the minotaur standing at the exit; then it charged. The beast charged slower this time, giving the couple time to dive out of the way again.

The injured beast now took longer to stop as well, which gave both Shiela and Grawn a chance to scramble back to their feet before it spun around and charged again.

It charged for Grawn again, and Grawn, prepared this time for his massive foe, recklessly charged as well.

The two were mere steps from each other and seconds away from Grawn's impaling when Grawn threw his heavy axe as hard as he could toward the massive beast.

The axe tumbled through the air and sank deep into the beast's shoulder.

The two were almost on top of each other, and as Grawn had hoped, the axe distracted the minotaur just long enough for Grawn to grab ahold of one of the beast's deadly horns. Using his momentum and body weight, Grawn jumped into a swing of sorts as the minotaur's own momentum carried it forward.

The beast roared in fury and pain from both the axe and Grawn's assault as Grawn let his momentum carry him back;

then when he felt his momentum at the peak of its power, he yanked as hard as he could.

He heard a resounding crack, and the beast fell silent in mid-roar, its body falling limp to the ground.

Grawn landed with a painful thud on the cold stone floor. Ignoring the pain, he lay there waiting. The monster lay still and silent, and when Grawn was satisfied he had indeed killed the beast, he stood to his feet and retrieved his axe from the its shoulder, then made his way over to Shiela, who stood heavy on her good leg, leaning on her bow for support.

The guiding orb returned to eye level and dimmed once again then moved toward the alcove exit. The red light glowed once more, then flashed, and the dead minotaur appeared in the alcove. Shiela and Grawn, prepared this time for the blinding light, turned away from the flash, and when they turned back, they noticed both the lifeless minotaur as well as the orb floating past the alcove then fall to the stone floor with a clang, its light suddenly going out.

"Well, I guess that means we are through this terrible labyrinth," Shiela said.

"Let us hope," Grawn replied.

"Well, let's get out of this place, and then we can find a place to rest," Shiela said.

Grawn nodded, and the two made their way to the exit, Grawn snatching up Shiela's arrows for her.

The aura around them shifted the moment they left the confines of the maze. Their fear lifted instantly, and the night air seemed fresher.

They had become so used to fighting with the unnatural fear that they suddenly felt like they could take on an entire army of orcs. They felt lighter and more relaxed immediately.

Grawn saw the orb and snatched it up, then noticed the great black tower looming before them. Shiela had stopped already, admiring the towering building ahead of them.

It was still a mile or more away, but the menacing building with the winged guards around it silhouetted against the moon behind it brought a measure of trepidation to the couple, though it paled in comparison to the unnatural fear they had become accustomed to in the maze.

"Let's not go there just yet," Shiela said.

"I will search for a place to make camp," Grawn replied and disappeared into the shadows. He returned minutes later.

"There are some ruins that will serve as well as any place for a camp. We can even make a fire," he said.

"Okay, show me the way; I'll take first watch." Grawn nodded and led her to the ruins.

They made camp quickly; Grawn was asleep before the fire fully caught, and Shiela kept alert for any hints of danger. A few hours later, Shiela woke Grawn for his watch and she too was asleep in minutes while Grawn paced back and forth, keeping his senses alert.

Dawn broke, and the two were off toward the black tower shortly after Shiela woke. She had slept well past dawn and didn't wake until the sun broke through the trees, shining right into her eyes.

They traveled slowly due to Shiela's leg. She could walk better now that she had rested and given her leg a few hours to heal. Her entire calf was bruised and sore to the touch, and every step was painful, but she was no stranger to pain, so she gritted her teeth and kept walking.

Grawn's own wound throbbed as well, still not healing well due to the constant activity, but he too was no stranger to pain and gritted his teeth as well and kept on.

When they finally stepped out into the open perimeter of the looming black tower, they instantly forgot about their pain as half a dozen shrieks pierced the silence surrounding them, and the flying tower guards swooped down on them.

-Find out what happened before the *Labyrinth* in *The King's Daughter Part 2: A Quest Begins* in book 3.

-If you liked the book, please leave a review on the store

website that you bought the book.

-Visit C. J. Korryn's website for more of his books.

https://www.cjkorryn.com/books

Sign up for C.J. Korryn's newsletter

https://authorcjkorryn.wixsite.com/mailinglist

Check out C. J. Korryn's Serial novels on Patreon

https://patreon.com/cjkorryn

Connect with C. J. Korryn through:

<u>Website:</u>

https://www.cjkorryn.com/

<u>Blog</u>:

https://authorcjkorryn.wixsite.com/blog

<u>Twitter</u>:

https://twitter.com/cjkorryn

<u>Facebook</u>:

https://www.facebook.com/AUTHORCJKORRYN/

<u>Instagram</u>:

https://WWW.instagram.com/cjkorryn/

www.ingramcontent.com/pod-product-compliance
Lightning Source LLC
Chambersburg PA
CBHW071540100726

47908CB00004B/1450